Beware the Shadow Phoenix

The Junior Novelization

ISBN 978-0-449-81775-9

randomhouse.com/kids

Printed in the United States of America

10 9 8 7 6 5 4 3 2 1

Beware the Shadow Phoenix

The Junior Novelization

Adapted by J. E. Bright

Random House New York

CHAPTER 1

Bloom smiled up at the late-afternoon sunshine. It had been a gorgeous day at Alfea College for Fairies. The shimmering pink walls of the school curved around its beautiful courtyard, where Bloom reclined on the steps leading to the main castle. The pretty, scarlet-haired fairy could barely remember when she had last felt so relaxed, and her emerald eyes sparkled with happiness.

Best of all, a few of the guys, friends known as the Specialists, had flown over in their spacecraft from the nearby school for wizards, Redfountain. Bloom loved Alfea, her friends the Winx, and being a powerful magical fairy, but there was something extra special about hanging out with the Specialist Prince Sky. He was just so sweet and strong and

brave . . . and the fact that he was blond and dashingly handsome didn't hurt, either.

"Isn't it great to have everything back to normal?" asked Sky, leaning against the staircase beside Bloom.

Bloom smiled. "You mean no invading armies?" she joked. "No monsters, no . . . Trix?" She shuddered as she remembered the past couple of days. A trio of nasty witches who called themselves the Trix had stolen Bloom's powers and built a horrifying army of darkness. First they'd taken over the witches' college, Cloudtower, and then they'd overrun Redfountain. The Trix had gone mad with desire to rule the Magic Dimension, and their army had swelled until it was the largest invasion the enchanted land of Magix had seen for generations.

The witches, the Specialists, and the fairies had all made a valiant stand at Alfea, holding off the Trix and their army until the Winx could help Bloom regain her fairy powers.

When she got her powers back, Bloom became mightier that she had ever dreamed. In the intense pressure of the battle with the Trix, Bloom discovered

that she could conjure up the Power of Dragon Flame. She'd created an enormous dragon made of fire that dwarfed the entire fairy college. With luck, cleverness, and bravery—and a lot of help from the Winx and the other students and teachers of Magix—Bloom had defeated the three Trix: Stormy, Darcy, and Icy. The Trix's army had dissolved into purple goo, and the evil witches were banished to a monastery in another dimension.

"Yeah," said Sky, interrupting Bloom's thoughts. He grinned at her. "Just chilling, you and me—"

"And all of our friends," added Bloom with a giggle. She waved her finger toward the other side of the wide stairs, where her best friend, Stella, stood, talking animatedly to Flora, Musa, Brandon, and Riven.

"Furthermore," Stella told her friends, "if it were up to me, they would lock up those Trix and throw away the key."

Riven was wearing a sleeveless shirt that showed off his arms. He looked a little bored, but Flora and Brandon were listening intently to Stella.

Putting her hands on her hips, Stella turned to greet Tecna and Timmy as they walked over. "Hey!" she called cheerfully.

Timmy's eyeglasses reflected the orange-and-purple sunset as he placed a hand on Tecna's back. "Isn't it great that we can all be together?" he said, smiling.

Elsewhere, a chestnut-haired teenage fairy named Aisha was feeling a lot less relaxed. She grunted as she climbed the jagged rock wall of a narrow underground tower.

The tower rose hundreds of feet into the heart of a vast subterranean cavern. Almost hidden by massive stalactites hanging from the ceiling of the cave, a small castle was perched on top of the tower, cut from the twisted rock. All around it, giant waterfalls gushed from the ceiling to the lake far below.

Aisha groaned as she reached a ledge just a few yards beneath the castle, panting from the effort of

climbing so far. "The Pixies," she gasped, urging herself to keep going. "I can't give up! I have to get to the Pixies."

With a final burst of energy, Aisha found a foothold in the rock with her boot and pushed herself upward, scaling chunky boulders until she managed to get her upper body and then her knee onto the flat ledge. She rolled onto it and sat up, her chest heaving.

As Aisha raised her arm to wipe her brow, she heard a familiar squeaky voice nearby. She glanced around and spotted a fiery glow in a stone passage into the tower. Aisha sighed with relief. She'd finally managed to reach her destination at the bottom level of the castle—the dungeons.

"We must all promise," said the high-pitched voice. Aisha thought it might belong to her friend Lockette, and she climbed wearily to her feet and headed into the tunnel, following the sound.

"Everybody!" another high-pitched voice insisted. "Promise!" That sounded to Aisha like her friend Digit, so she hurried faster along the tunnel.

When Aisha turned a corner, she found glowing pillars of magical plasma in a stone chamber. Seven of her Pixie friends were floating inside one of the shimmering pillars. She could see Lockette, Digit, Zing, Tune, Amore, Piff, and Chatta. The Pixies were imprisoned in the plasma column, but they seemed unhurt.

"We will never show the Phoenix the way to Pixie Village," swore Chatta, bobbing in the twinkling plasma of the pillar. "Never. Never, ever, ever."

Zing turned her head when she heard Aisha's footsteps. Her mask and antennae made her look like an adorable bumblebee. "Shh," she said to the others. "Quiet. Someone's coming."

When Aisha stepped into the stone chamber, they gasped happily, thrilled to see their friend.

"Aisha!" Amore cried. She had rosebuds on pigtail bows in her pink hair. "Oh! You've come to get us!"

Aisha knelt so that she was face to face with the little Pixies. "Of course," she said solemnly. "I wouldn't leave you here."

Lockette, a Pixie with a bobbed helmet of purple hair, pointed to a carved slab nearby. "The lock is on that wall," she peeped.

When Aisha saw that the wall was decorated with statues of skeletal monsters and dragons, she flinched in fear. As she scanned the wall, she noticed that one of the carved lizards near the ceiling had eyes that blinked with a red radiance.

"Maybe . . . ," Aisha muttered, wondering how she could unfasten the magical lock with her powers. She held up her hand and it glowed softly with purple energy. She quickly created a brilliant sphere of power and flung it at the glowing dragon's eyes.

The purple sphere hit the lock, which sizzled with sparks.

Seconds later, the plasma pillars disappeared into the stone floor. As Aisha panted from the effort of using her powers, the seven Pixies crashed to the ground.

Aisha gathered the Pixies in her arms and stood up. "Everybody ready?" she asked.

"Yes!" they chirped.

Holding the Pixies carefully against her chest, Aisha hastened down a murky corridor away from the dungeon. "We've got to find a way out of here," she said, "and fast!"

While she hurried down the hall, Piff, a Pixie wearing a pale pink bonnet, climbed up Aisha's shoulder and hid in the hood of her sweater-vest.

Aisha ran down the corridor, unaware that an evil creature was watching her magically from his lair high in the tower.

The creature looked like a mix between a tall demon and a lobster, with a reddish outline of energy buzzing all around him. He had sharp claws, spikes sticking out of his back and shoulders, and red armor covering his head, chest, and hips. His neck, forearms, abdomen, and lower legs were just bones. His eyes burned in his helmet like hot coals.

"Run as fast as you can, foolish girl," the creature sneered. "But I see all. You and your Pixie friends will never escape me, the Shadow Phoenix!"

As the Shadow Phoenix let out an evil laugh, he

raised his hands. They blazed with red-hot force.

"Arise, shadow monsters!" he bellowed.

On the stone floor of the Shadow Phoenix's lair, three wisps of smoke appeared and twisted into grotesque black shapes. The red energy from the Shadow Phoenix's hands shaped the smoke, forcing it to grow larger and solidify into horrible creatures of darkness.

One gray beast looked like an eyeless, carnivorous dinosaur walking on its hind legs. Another was toxic green and bristling with spikes. The third was purple and sinuous like a snake but had multiple legs along its slithery body and many sharp teeth. The three monsters howled and drooled as they awaited further instruction from their master.

The Shadow Phoenix nodded, pleased with the abominations he had summoned. "Go," he ordered the beasts, "and seek out your prey!"

CHAPTER 2

Still cradling the Pixies in her arms, Aisha raced through the ornate corridors of the Shadow Phoenix's castle. She flung open a set of huge swinging doors, hoping she'd found the exit. But behind the doors was a dark, dank circular chamber filled with dusty old furniture. The narrow windows in the room were all secured with iron bars. Aisha nervously entered the chamber.

In a burst of fiery energy, a heap of mud appeared in the middle of the chamber. The ooze morphed into the biggest shadow monster, the one that looked like an eyeless tyrannosaurus. It roared at Aisha, and she and the Pixies screamed in terror. They screamed again when Aisha spun around and saw the other two shadow monsters lurking behind her.

The spiny monster leapt and Aisha tumbled away, still holding the Pixies. Chatta fell out of her arms but managed to grab on to a trailing tendril of the fairy's long hair.

"Whoa!" Chatta shrieked, gripping Aisha's hair desperately.

The leggy snake monster lurched forward and snapped at Aisha. Without a second's hesitation, Aisha flipped high over the beast, landed on her feet, and raced ahead. Somehow all the Pixies managed to hang on while Aisha escaped.

With the Pixies screaming in her arms, Aisha fled along the corridor until she reached a narrow set of double doors. But on the other side of the doors was a thick stone ledge . . . on the outside wall of the castle! Aisha stopped short when she saw the steep drop in front of her. Below lay the depths of the enormous cavern around the castle, at the bottom of which was a lake . . . far, far down. A narrow bridge connected the castle to a distant point across the cavern.

That bridge doesn't look safe at all, Aisha thought breathlessly. She considered trying to climb down the giant stalagmite that the castle sat on, but there was

no way she could manage the difficult descent while carrying the Pixies she'd rescued.

Before Aisha could decide whether to risk the bridge or try climbing down, an enormous burning bird soared overhead, flapping its flaming wings. The massive bird howled at Aisha, and she gasped in fear.

"Oh, no!" squealed Chatta. "It's the Phoenix!"

"Run!" Tune screamed.

The Shadow Phoenix twisted in the air as he dropped to the wide ledge, and after he'd landed, he crouched down, covering himself with his wings. When he opened his wings again, he stood on two legs, transformed into his armored humanoid shape.

He strode toward Aisha angrily. "You can't escape," the Phoenix growled, holding out an open hand that ended in five finger-like claws. "Hand over the Pixies!"

"Never!" Aisha cried. "I won't let you have them!"

"Wrong answer," said the Phoenix. He flipped his hand up and his palm glowed with eerie red power. He launched a sphere of burning energy, knocking

Aisha to the stone ledge. The Pixies flew out of Aisha's arms, scattering around her.

The same sphere of crimson energy that had blasted Aisha encircled six of the seven Pixies. The energy bobbed in the air for a moment, securing the captured Pixies, then rocketed back to the Shadow Phoenix.

Piff, who had been riding in Aisha's hood, tried to stay hidden. She was the only Pixie who hadn't been snagged by the energy sphere. But she let out a whimper of fear when she saw the Shadow Phoenix raise one of his sharp skeleton claws, ready to slash Aisha where she lay on the ground.

As the Shadow Phoenix swung his claw, Aisha narrowed her eyes in determination. She conjured up shimmering purple magic that swirled into a circular shield above her. The Shadow Phoenix's pointed nails pierced Aisha's shield, but the shield was strong; he couldn't reach her or Piff.

The Shadow Phoenix stood up to his full imposing height. "Fighting back?" he sneered. "How foolish."

Aisha groaned, struggling to climb to her feet. She stood and squared her shoulders. "A fairy never gives up without a fight!" she declared.

"Very well, then," replied the Shadow Phoenix. He stretched out an arm and launched a sizzling energy blast at Aisha.

Aisha tumbled out of the way, which only angered the Shadow Phoenix. His eyes glowed red as he clenched one hand. All around his tense fist, squiggles of gray shadow squirmed and then suddenly reached out toward Aisha. The shadowy tentacles grabbed Aisha's arms and she screamed, struggling to break free. But the tentacles were too strong, and they lifted her off the ledge, dangling her over the perilous drop.

The Shadow Phoenix laughed nastily. "Goodbye, fairy," he said, and the tentacles let Aisha go.

Aisha cried out in terror as she plummeted off the tower toward the cavern's lake far below.

♥ ♥ ♥

A few hours later, the Winx stood in Alfea's courtyard and waved to Sky, Brandon, Riven, and Timmy. The four Specialists took off in their ship, returning to Redfountain.

"Goodbye!" called Stella.

"Bye, Sky!" shouted Bloom as the spacecraft flew off over the forest on the outskirts of Alfea.

Bloom watched the departing spacecraft with a happy grin. Flora peered into the woods and crossed her arms worriedly. "Bloom," she said, "I think there's something in the trees." Bloom followed Flora's gaze into the forest and saw someone stumbling out at the edge of the tree line.

"Bye, Brandon!" called Stella, still waving to the Specialists, who were now out of sight. She stopped waving when Bloom hurried past her. "Hey," the blond fairy asked worriedly, "where are you going?"

Bloom stepped closer to the forest's edge, on high alert, ready to protect the school if the new person turned out to be dangerous.

Then the person stepped into the evening sunlight.

A teenage fairy, looking exhausted and bedraggled, stumbled onto the grounds of Alfea. She had messy chestnut hair, and her pink sweater-vest was soiled and torn. Her legs wobbled on the lawn, and her eyes brimmed with tears.

"Oh!" gasped Bloom. "Are you okay?"

The strange fairy shivered and tripped. "Uh . . . ," she moaned, and then she fainted. Bloom rushed forward, catching her when she fell.

The other Winx hurried over as Bloom gently laid the fairy on the grass and cradled her head in her lap. Musa held one of the fairy's hands.

"Come on," Bloom whispered, "wake up." She brushed the unconscious fairy's long hair with her fingers . . . and a small creature fell out of her hood and bounced softly onto the lawn.

Stella stared at the tiny sleeping creature on the grass. It was wearing a pink bonnet and white pantaloons. "What is it?" she asked.

Her eyes wide with amazement, Bloom picked up the little creature. "I think it's a Pixie," she breathed.

Holding the Pixie, Bloom knelt beside the

unconscious fairy, trying to figure out how she had gotten to Alfea in such a vulnerable state.

"Who is this girl?" Bloom wondered aloud to the other Winx. "What could have happened to her?"

Chapter
3

The next morning, the strange fairy awoke in Alfea's cozy infirmary. She gasped and sat up abruptly, glancing in shock at Musa and Bloom perched on the edge of her bed. "Where am I?" she asked. She pressed her palm against her forehead. "Oh, no . . . the Pixies!"

Flora stepped closer, smiling down at the fairy reassuringly. "You're safe," she said, "at Alfea." Flora gently placed a cool, damp cloth on the fairy's brow. "This will help with the headache."

"Oh," the young fairy murmured, looking a little less panicked.

Bloom scooted closer to her. "Can you tell us what happened?" she asked.

Before the fairy could answer, Flora handed her

a mug of steaming medicinal tea. "Here," she said, "drink this. It will help you get your strength back."

"Thanks," said the fairy. She sipped the tea, and some color returned to her cheeks. "My name is Aisha," she said. "I was in Gloomywood on my way to visit my friends the Pixies, when two of them found me. They told me that horrible shadow monsters had captured some Pixies. I followed the trail the creatures left. It took me deep underground until I reached . . . the castle of the Shadow Phoenix."

"The Shadow Phoenix?" asked Bloom.

"Who's the Shadow Phoenix?" Stella chimed in.

Aisha lowered her head, trembling with emotion. "Sometimes he looks like an ancient warrior in bloodred armor," she said, shivering. "And sometimes he's a giant bird of prey." Tears trailed down her face, and she brushed them away with her fingertips. "He took the Pixies captive. I tried to save them, but . . ." She let out a big sob. "I should have never left them!"

Beside her, Musa opened her arms. "Come here," she said, and she hugged Aisha, who wept.

Bloom placed a hand on Aisha's heaving back.

"We'll help you rescue the Pixies," she swore.

Musa gave Aisha a squeeze and then stepped back to look directly into Aisha's tear-filled eyes with a warm smile. "You can count on us," she promised.

On a pillow behind Aisha on the bed, the little Pixie Piff slept on, softly snoring.

"Thank you," said Aisha, wiping her eyes as she gazed at the sleeping Piff.

The isolated Lightrock Monastery was situated on a lush mountaintop so high that its base was buried in the thick surrounding clouds. The beautiful sandstone castle was a place of peace and internal reflection, where spiritual people went to commune with Infinity.

It was also the place where the wicked Trix had been sent as punishment for trying to take over the Magic Dimension. Despite the calming influence of their beautiful surroundings, Icy, Darcy, and Stormy were as nasty as ever.

From where she was sulking, slumped sideways

across a hammock, the white-haired Icy glared at the beautifully tended grounds of the monastery and the quiet residents lounging in the lovely setting. She was wearing an unflattering beige robe, just like everyone else at Lightrock. Icy let out a big, frustrated sigh of boredom as she flashed hateful looks at a cute couple chatting on a quaint bench, at a young man reading quietly by a flower garden, and at other people sitting calmly in the rolling green hills of the pretty landscape.

Not far away, Stormy was sitting under a gorgeous tree blooming with thousands of pastel-colored flowers. As the petals fell, swirling down to land gently in Stormy's hair, the young witch growled with barely contained rage.

Darcy lay on her back on a large flat rock between the other two Trix. "Go away," she hissed at the couple on the bench, and their image flickered and fizzled out. They had only been holograms. "Ugh," groaned Darcy. "They were driving me crazy."

Icy echoed Darcy's groan. "I just don't know how much more of this I can take."

The bright sunny day suddenly fell into shadow,

making Icy glance upward. She was surprised to see clouds darkening the sky, turning it charcoal gray, highlighted by a sickly crimson glow behind them. Jagged purple lightning flashed. Icy pushed herself off the hammock. "What's happening?"

"I don't know," Stormy said as lightning streaked across the dark sky again. "But I like it."

"Yes," Icy said, smiling. A hot wind began to whip her hair around. "Something wicked is in the air."

An ugly scarlet tear in the sky appeared in front of the three witches, revealing a doorway between dimensions. The Shadow Phoenix strode through the magic portal onto the grounds of Lightrock Monastery and headed directly toward the Trix.

"Oh, *my*," Icy said, raising an eyebrow appreciatively.

"Come with me," the Shadow Phoenix said. He raised his arms, and his tattered cape flapped in the wind. "I have need of your dark hearts."

Icy smiled and walked toward the huge, evil beast. "Am I ever pleased to hear that," she said, leading

Darcy and Stormy into the Shadow Phoenix's embrace.

The Shadow Phoenix closed his shredded cape around the three witches, and with a sinister *whoosh*, they were transported away from their painfully pleasant prison and back to the Magic Dimension.

It wasn't long before they arrived in the throne room deep in the dark heart of the Shadow Phoenix's underground castle. Behind them was a dais, where an enormous statue of a skeletal snake loomed above the spiky throne, rearing up to the cavernous ceiling.

"Now, my dear Trix," the Shadow Phoenix said with a nasty chuckle, "I will give you a gift." He raised one bony arm and three spheres of purple and green light danced in swirls above his palm. "The gift of invincible power!"

As he concentrated on the spinning spheres, an ornate purple bracelet materialized around Darcy's wrist, shimmering with cold energy. An identical

bracelet appeared around Stormy's arm, and a delicate necklace of glowing green glittered brilliantly around Icy's neck. With the powerful jewelry in place, the witches struck gleeful poses as they were bathed in waves of pulsating purple force.

Thrilled with the power the Shadow Phoenix had shared with them, the Trix knelt before him, swearing their allegiance to the demonic beast.

"Now you serve me, the Shadow Phoenix," he growled, standing on the dais before his new minions.

"Yes, master," the Trix said in unison, bowing their heads.

"Soon I will rule the whole Magic Dimension," said the Shadow Phoenix. "But first I must have the Codex. And you are going to get it for me."

Still kneeling, the Trix nodded, grinning. "Yes, master," they said again.

"The Pixies have it in their village," the Shadow Phoenix continued, "which is hidden to all but them. They will never tell me where it is. But I have a plan to find Pixie Village and seize the Codex . . . and

those Winx fairies are going to help me!" He held up his arms, and in a flash of purple, an image of the fairies in a classroom at Alfea appeared between his menacing hands.

Chapter 4

In that same classroom at Alfea, Headmistress Faragonda stood in front of the clean blackboard, addressing Aisha and the Winx, who were sitting at desks in the front row.

"My dear girls," said Miss Faragonda, clasping her hands in front of herself primly, "from all that Aisha has told us, it is clear that we are facing a new evil." The older fairy began to pace along the front of the room. "We must act," she said, stroking her chin thoughtfully. "We must free the Pixies at once."

"Do we need to enter the Phoenix's underground castle?" asked Bloom.

"Yes," Miss Faragonda replied. She placed a hand on Aisha's shoulder. "We know where our enemy is,

but we do not know exactly *who* he is." She peered at the Winx over her small triangular spectacles. "We must be inconspicuous. Piff will stay at Alfea. Only Bloom and Stella will go with Aisha," she said decidedly. "Timmy will take you there."

Immediately, the fairies and their headmistress set their plan in action. They got in contact with the Specialists, who were happy to send a spacecraft with Timmy as their pilot. Without delay, Bloom, Stella, and Aisha found themselves inside Timmy's spaceship, zooming over the forest.

"I'm heading straight for the valley you told us about," Timmy informed Aisha as he steered the ship along the slope of a tree-lined hill. Timmy was the brainiest of the Specialists. He was a little nerdy, and he wore unflattering glasses, but he was sweet and cute in his own way. "We should be there in just a few minutes."

In the ship's cockpit, Stella, Bloom, and Aisha peered out the front window.

Aisha pointed at a dark spot on the hillside. "There it is," she said. "That's the entrance to the

cave." Then she pointed to a deep valley near the opening. "You should set us down over there."

"Are you sure I can't get you any closer?" asked Timmy.

"No," Aisha replied. "We don't want the Phoenix to know we're coming."

Little did she know, as the spaceship lowered for landing, the Shadow Phoenix was spying on their approach through one of his energy spheres.

"Just as I planned," the Shadow Phoenix growled. He clenched his fist, making the vision of the spaceship in the energy sphere disappear. Then he paced around his throne room, deciding his next move. "I think I will send the Trix to welcome our visitors!"

The Shadow Phoenix let out a deep, booming laugh as he conjured up another energy sphere. He peered into it and an image of Aisha, Bloom, and Stella came into focus.

♥ ♥ ♥

Bloom and Stella stood on a rocky ledge, waving goodbye to Timmy's ship, as Aisha marched into the cave entrance.

"Follow me," Aisha called to Stella and Bloom. "This is the way in."

The three fairies ducked into the small entrance and hurried into a long tunnel carved into the mountainside. They were all wearing khaki safari outfits, ready for their mission. Bloom and Stella followed Aisha into a winding corridor, deeper into the underground world.

"Come on," urged Aisha. "It's not much farther."

They exited the tunnel and arrived in a vast cavern. Aisha paused at the start of a narrow rope-and-wood bridge that wobbled across a deep chasm. "If we move fast, maybe we can get to the Pixies before the Shadow Phoenix even knows we're here."

"That would be nice," said Stella. Before she followed Aisha onto the flimsy bridge, Stella peered up at the castle. The bridge connected to the castle's base, and the entrance looked extremely unwelcoming.

With a deep breath, Stella stepped onto the bridge. Bloom was beside her. The wooden slats creaked ominously no matter how carefully the fairies placed their feet.

"Hurry up, you guys!" Aisha called, already on the other side.

Stella felt light-headed and had to pause to hold on to one of the bridge's swinging rope sides. "There's no sunshine here," she whimpered. "It's making me feel a little weak." As the Fairy of the Shining Sun, she was happiest soaking up solar rays.

Aisha grew impatient waiting for Bloom and Stella. She grabbed for a rope attached to the castle's front tower. "I'm going on ahead!" she called.

Stella let out a little gasp of surprise as Aisha jumped off the side of the bridge and swung across the deep cavern to the dungeon level of the castle. When the rope got to the end of its arc, Aisha flung herself onto a stone ledge and reached for a column.

With a grunt, she hoisted herself up onto the column and dropped into the dungeon.

"Aisha!" the six Pixies exclaimed from their plasma prison.

Aisha raced over to the column of plasma and knelt in front of the Pixies so she was at their level.

"I knew you would come back for us!" peeped Chatta.

Aisha wiggled her fingers at the Pixies in greeting. "Time to get you guys out of here!" she said.

Meanwhile, back on the bridge, Stella was still clinging to the rope, barely keeping her balance.

When Bloom reached the stone ledge at the castle, she called back to Stella, "Are you all right?"

"Yeah!" Stella said, faking a cheerful tone. "Feeling . . . great. I'll be there in just a sec."

Bloom nodded. "I'm going to catch up with Aisha," she said, but just as she turned around to head into the dungeon, a bolt of lightning struck her, blasting her off her feet. She rolled onto the stone ledge and held her head as she sat up.

Icy, Stormy, and Darcy lowered themselves from the air onto the ledge. All three Trix had their hands on their hips, and they smirked at Bloom and Stella.

Bloom stared at the glowing purple bracelets on Stormy and Darcy, and the brilliant green necklace

Icy wore. "What are those things?" she muttered to herself.

"The Trix!" gasped Stella.

Bloom jumped to her feet, ready to fight. "Stella," she shouted. "Transform!"

"Magic Winx!" Stella and Bloom yelled in unison. "Charmix!"

Stella spun around as brilliant yellow energy exploded all around her. "Stella!" she shouted as her outfit transformed into a snug and shimmering orange battle uniform, and a power staff appeared in her hand. "Fairy of the Shining Sun!"

Then it was Bloom's turn to initiate her powers and change into her own magical form. "Bloom!" she cheered as red swirls of fiery force whirled around her. "Fairy of Dragon Flame!"

Bloom and Stella hovered above the ledge on their fluttering wings, listening to the Trix laughing. While the fairies were busy transforming, the witches had vanished into the shadows.

"I don't see them," said Bloom.

Stella peered around the base of the castle. "Where did they go?"

Then Stormy stepped into view, waving her arms. "Shadow Whirlwind!" she shouted, and a big purple tornado materialized in front of her. Jagged lightning flashed along its funnel, twisting toward Stella.

The sunny fairy held the tornado back for a second with her staff, but Stormy's attack was too powerful for her to fight for long. The tornado knocked her out of the air, and she landed hard on the stone ledge. She was out cold.

"Stella!" cried Bloom. She started to swoop down to her fallen friend, but Darcy raised a single finger and shot out concentric circles of purple force. The spiraling circles smacked into Bloom, slamming her back against a rock wall and knocking her unconscious.

Darcy laughed in evil glee. "The Shadow Phoenix was right," she said, gloating over the strength the glowing bracelet gave her.

"Sisters," said Icy, "we're better than ever."

Above the Trix, Aisha leapt onto a stone landing, transforming into her battle dress mid-jump. Sparkles of magical energy flew from her glittering yellow outfit. "Aisha, Fairy of the Waves!" she cried,

announcing herself to the Trix. Her fairy wings fluttered behind her. "Hey!" she yelled at the witches. "It's not over yet!" She wound up her arm and hurled a glowing purple sphere like she was pitching a softball.

Icy calmly reached out, grabbed Aisha's sphere in one hand, and squished it with almost no effort.

"Actually," Icy said with a chilling smile, "it is."

Chapter 5

Aisha jumped and landed on the stone ledge, her brow furrowed in concentration as she prepared her next move. Darcy abruptly teleported: she winked out from where she had been standing beside Icy and materialized behind Aisha.

Focusing her power, Darcy summoned purple pinwheels to radiate from her palms. She brought her hands together and the swirls combined to become a ray of circles that slammed into the back of Aisha's head, throwing her to the rocky ground. Aisha's glittery yellow battle outfit transformed back into her basic khaki clothes.

"Ha!" barked Darcy, pleased with how simple it had been to knock Aisha unconscious.

and Icy joined Darcy, hovering above

e work, Darcy!" said Icy.

the Trix's celebration was short-lived. Suddenly, a man appeared over their heads, unfurling huge golden wings behind him. He was dressed like a warrior of light, his cape, boots, and feathers shining so brilliantly that they blinded the witches. the Trix squealed in pain, shielding their eyes with their arms, but that did little to protect them.

"Who *is* that?" demanded Icy.

"This light!" Darcy whined. "I can't see anything!"

"What's going on?" asked Stormy, her voice edged with panic.

The luminous winged man flew over to where Aisha was slumped on the ledge. He landed and knelt beside the fallen fairy, holding a hand over her back. Softly glowing power healed her Aisha's wounds.

As Aisha stirred, the handsome warrior soared to Bloom, who was unconscious and floating in midair. He caught her in his arms, holding her gently until

she recovered, and then he lowered her safely to the ground.

Next, the winged man flew to Stella and healed her with a wave of his radiant hand.

Stella fluttered her eyes open, and she smiled when she saw the man's glowing face. "Would you look at that?" she said, sighing happily as the brilliant warrior flew back toward the Trix.

The shining man's wings blinded the witches again, and they cowered on the ground in front of him. He raised his arms and conjured up a gleaming yellow sphere above his hands. *"Vera captugan strigas seferune!"* he chanted, and hurled the sphere at the Trix. It blazed bigger as it slammed into them, encapsulating them in its glow.

The warrior pointed two fingers at the sphere and then cut his hand sharply to the side. The sphere followed his gesture, zipping out of the cavern, carrying the witches with it. The Trix screamed as they zoomed away in the sphere and disappeared.

Bloom, Stella, and Aisha cheered, thrilled to see the witches vanquished so easily.

"Thanks!" said Bloom.

In response, the shining warrior bowed deeply to the fairies, stretching out his wings. Then he leapt into the air and soared away until he was lost from view in the vast cavern.

"Wow," murmured Stella.

"Aisha!" squealed a group of high-pitched voices.

Aisha glanced around and hurried toward the source of the sound. "The Pixies!" she cried.

Miraculously freed from their dungeon, the six Pixies flew as fast as their little wings could carry them, joyfully crying out Aisha's name.

"Wait a minute!" Aisha said nervously when she saw how fast they were flying toward her. Bloom and Stella winced when the Pixies slammed into Aisha, knocking her to the ground as they squealed and giggled in delight.

Aisha managed to sit up with Pixies clinging to her hair and shoulders. "Pixies," she said, "these are my new friends, Bloom and Stella." She turned to smile at the fairies.

A Pixie wearing a purple gown flew off Aisha's head with her tiny green wings and hovered in front of Stella. "I am Amore," the Pixie chirped, patting the purple roses in her hair. "The Pixie of Feelings!"

"Oh!" Stella gasped, beaming at Amore. "You're wonderful!"

A Pixie with purple bobbed hair zipped over to Bloom. "Hi!" she peeped. "I'm Lockette, the Pixie of Direction!"

Bloom held out her palm, and Lockette landed on it.

"And I'm Bloom," the flame-haired fairy said, grinning at the little Pixie.

Aisha and the other Pixies smiled as they watched Bloom chatting with Lockette and Stella snuggling with Amore.

"They're bonding!" peeped Digit.

"Yes," Aisha breathed, awed at witnessing such wondrous magic between Pixies and fairies. "It's like love at first sight. And now their bond is unbreakable."

With the rescued Pixies, Aisha, Bloom, and Stella

hurried out of the castle and across the bridge. They exited the cavern the same way they'd come in, and found Timmy waiting for them in his spaceship.

Dusk was falling when Timmy landed the ship in Alfea's wide courtyard. Flora, Musa, and Tecna raced to the ship to greet their friends.

"Hey!" Flora cried. "Here they are!"

"All right!" cheered Musa.

Tecna pumped her fist. "Yeah!"

The door to the ship slid open, and Bloom, Stella, and Aisha ran out. All the fairies hugged one another, laughing. Little pink Piff hugged Aisha's face.

Then the newly rescued Pixies buzzed out of Timmy's spaceship. "Hello, hello, hello!" they squealed.

A Pixie wearing a green helmet zipped over to Tecna. "Greetings!" the Pixie said, peering at Tecna's handheld computer. "I am Digit."

Tune, a Pixie in a green dress with her purple hair

in tight curls, flew over to Musa. "Hello," Musa said, touching her fingers to the Pixie's hands.

"You rock!" chirped Tune.

Then Chatta, with her orange pigtails, swooped around Flora's head. "Hello, Flora!" she peeped. "I'm so happy to meet you. So, so happy!"

Flora hugged the little Pixie tight and giggled with joy.

Chapter
6

The reunited Winx immediately took the Pixies to Headmistress Faragonda's spacious office, where they gathered in front of her ornate desk. A multitasker, the headmistress continued to sort papers while she spoke to her students and their new friends. "I am delighted that you are back—with the Pixies! But we are not yet out of the woods, girls. If this Shadow Phoenix is looking for their village, the Pixies can't return there."

Miss Faragonda walked around her big desk and approached Aisha. "So, Aisha," she said, "I have spoken to your parents, and they agree that you and the Pixies should stay here at Alfea for the time being."

The Winx cheered at Miss Faragonda's announcement, jumping up and down excitedly.

"Thank you, Headmistress Faragonda," said Aisha, nodding solemnly. She felt honored to be under the protection of the fairy college and its powerful headmistress.

Miss Faragonda paced over to the large picture windows behind her desk. "I know we can keep you all safe," she said. "And to help, let me introduce . . . Professor Avalon." She waved her hand, and a tall man wearing a blue cloak with a hood appeared in the middle of her office.

The man smiled and pulled back his hood, revealing long salt-and-pepper hair and a handsome face that was completely familiar, even though at the moment it wasn't lit by the glow of his radiant wings.

"The winged man!" gasped Bloom.

Stella's mouth dropped open in surprise.

"He rescued us from the Trix!" said Aisha.

♥ ♥ ♥

Late that night, Bloom tossed in her bed, in the grip of a powerful dream. With the intensity of a surfacing distant memory, she dreamed she was a baby, waving her pudgy arms around her cradle, reaching for the silhouettes of her birth parents . . . and her sister, Daphne. Bloom was shocked at the realization of who they were—she had no recollection of ever meeting her family in her waking life. She'd been raised on Earth by her adoptive, nonmagical parents, whom she loved very much.

"Mom?" said Daphne in the dream. "Bloom's awake."

"Isn't she lovely?" Bloom's father asked.

"Aww," her mother cooed, leaning down to pick Bloom up out of the cradle. "Come here, darling—"

With a gasp, Bloom sat up in her bed, the dream shattering around her. She panted in the darkness for a long moment, trying to piece together the long-forgotten memory that had returned to her in the dream. She flopped back onto her pillow. "My birth parents," she whispered sadly, her eyes filling with tears. "My family."

She felt overwhelmed with loss, heartbroken that she hadn't known the people who had loved her as an infant. But there was also something wonderful about having had the quick vision of her parents and sister in the dream.

Bloom turned sideways in bed, curling up as she cried herself back to sleep, feeling both miserable and oddly comforted that she'd gotten a glimpse of her birth family at all.

♥ ♥ ♥

The next morning, the sun rose but didn't shine, hidden behind thick rain clouds. Alfea's grounds were sodden and gloomy in the bleak downpour.

The fairy students gathered for breakfast in the vast dining hall, grumbling with discontent. Usually, the giant windows in the hall sparkled with sunlight, igniting the crystal chandeliers overhead with dazzling rainbow refractions, but today the weather was dismal and drab.

Stella flopped down at the table she shared with the other Winx. "Oh, man!" she groaned, slumping and putting her head on her arms on the tabletop. "It's pouring and gray and utterly depressing. Life stinks."

A green stem suddenly appeared on the table in front of Stella's face. "Oh!" gasped Stella. The stem quickly bloomed into a beautiful violet iris. Stella sat up, her eyes wide with amazement, as a gorgeous flower materialized in front of each fairy's place setting, brightening up the atmosphere.

"Wow!" said Musa.

"Ahh!" breathed Flora. "Nice!"

Resplendent in a neat white suit, Professor Avalon strode into the dining hall, walking between the long tables of fairies, with the seven Pixies fluttering in the air near the Winx. "Good morning," he said.

"Good morning, Professor Avalon," everyone replied cheerfully.

"I hope the flowers got your day off to a cheery start," said the handsome teacher.

Bloom picked up her iris and sniffed it deeply.

"Thank you, Professor," she said. "Purple is my favorite color."

Beside Bloom, Flora piped up. "Yes, it's mine, too."

Professor Avalon stopped walking and looked at Bloom. His smile faded. His eyes became serious as he placed a hand on Bloom's shoulder. "I sense you are troubled," he said. "Perhaps about a dream you had."

"Oh," Bloom said, peering down at the iris in her hand. She felt the disturbing emotions of the dream surge through her heart. "I dreamed about my birth parents. I could hear their voices." She glanced up at the professor. "I want so much to know more about them."

"I think I can help you," Professor Avalon said. "Come to my office after class." Then he turned around and strode out of the dining hall.

Stella sniffed her flower and sighed happily. "Life is wonderful," she said.

"Best day ever," Musa agreed.

After Bloom was done with her morning class, she made her way to Professor Avalon's office. She and the professor chatted for a while, and he explained that he could help her by putting her in a calm mental state. Then she could remember her family better. He instructed Bloom to rest on a couch in his office. While small, radiant orbs floated above her, Bloom closed her eyes and let herself relax.

"Empty your mind of everything but the sound of my voice," said Professor Avalon.

"Yes, Professor," replied Bloom sleepily. "I'm listening."

"Good," said Professor Avalon. "Now fly, Bloom. . . ."

Bloom found herself floating in a dreamlike cloud, imagining beams of sunlight piercing the thick, swirling atmosphere. She was wearing her battle clothes, and her wings fluttered on her back.

"See your birth parents . . . ," Professor Avalon continued.

In Bloom's mystical vision, the clouds parted, revealing her mother and father standing and smiling at her, reaching toward her with outstretched arms.

Professor Avalon's voice added, "And your power . . ." Above her parents, Bloom noticed a crimson dragon looming in the sky, shimmering with fiery force.

"The dragon!" Bloom gasped, alarmed.

The dragon let out a terrifying roar, and dark swirls of smoke surrounded Bloom, blocking her from her parents.

"No!" cried Bloom, trying to fly closer. "Don't go!" The smoke covered her parents and the dragon. "What's happening?"

The smoke spun faster, whirling until a frightening, monstrous face appeared in the dark clouds. The monster snarled furiously at Bloom, and she covered her face with her hands in fear.

With a shriek, Bloom sat up on Professor Avalon's couch, blinking away the terrifying vision.

The glowing orbs fell out of the air around her, bouncing onto the floor and rolling away.

"What did you see, Bloom?" Professor Avalon asked.

Bloom turned and looked up at him. "I don't know," she replied. She closed her eyes for a moment, trying to recall the scary vision, but it remained stubbornly out of reach. "I . . . I can't remember."

"Don't worry," said Professor Avalon, smiling at her reassuringly. "In time it will be clear."

Chapter 7

The next day, Professor Avalon brought the fairies and the Pixies over to the Specialists' college. Redfountain had been demolished in the attack by the Trix's hideous army, but through the Specialists' tireless efforts, it had been completely rebuilt. A day of celebration had been planned to honor the school's reconstruction.

"Here we are, girls," Professor Avalon said to the fairies at the school's repaired entrance. "The opening of the new Redfountain."

In anticipation of the special event, Bloom had decided to wear a T-shirt with a heart printed on the front and fashionable tights under her skirt. "Thank

you so much for bringing us, Professor Avalon," she said. Three Pixies bobbed around her head in agreement.

"It's going to be a great day," the professor said. "Now enjoy yourselves. We'll all meet after the ceremony." He strode ahead into the Specialists' school, his long black-and-white ponytail swinging behind him.

"He's so great," Bloom said with a happy sigh.

Inside Redfountain's walls, the Winx met up with Sky, Brandon, Timmy, and Riven. The Winx gathered on a new bench as the boys chatted with them.

"I'm so glad you could make it," Sky told the girls. He bowed deeply. "Welcome to the new Redfountain."

The four Specialists gave the teenage fairies a tour of the fixed-up grounds, which now included new trees planted along the walkways to replace the ones the Trix's army had torn up.

"So," said Bloom as they walked through the beautiful landscape, "what do you guys have planned for the ceremony?"

Sky smiled. "It's going to be quite a surprise," he replied.

Lockette landed on Bloom's shoulder, holding on to the fairy's red hair. "I wonder where Professor Avalon is," said Bloom. "I wouldn't want him to miss the surprise."

Sky narrowed his eyes at the obvious admiration in Bloom's voice. "Who's Professor Avalon?" he asked, trying to keep his question casual.

"Oh, Sky," gushed Bloom. "He's the best." She suddenly bolted away, running through the crowd of her friends. "I'm going to find him. Meet you guys there!"

Sky watched her disappear down the pretty path he'd helped re-create. Then he let out a long, confused sigh and led the Specialists and the Winx toward the new stadium.

When they reached the rebuilt arena, Brandon hurried over to the bleachers, where a young Specialist was busy drawing pigeons in a notebook.

"Hey, Helia," Brandon called to the new student. "Meet the Winx." He gestured to the fairies. "Stella, Tecna—" he began.

"Hello," said Helia, standing up. He had long black hair in a loose ponytail and dark, serious eyes. He held up his notebook. "I was just doing some sketching."

Flora tilted her head to try to see his work, so Helia handed his notebook to her.

Flipping through the pages, Flora smiled. "Wow . . . you used the fern texture of the paper to make the birds' wings."

Helia's mouth opened slightly in his surprise. *Nobody ever notices the fern texture of the paper,* he thought in amazement.

"And this is Flora," Brandon said, concluding his introductions.

"Flora," repeated Helia, stunned.

Trumpets sounded around the stadium, and the Winx, the Pixies, and the Specialists took seats in the stands. All around them, Specialists and fairies waved flags and banners, and the crowd erupted with

cheers as the Specialists' headmaster, Mr. Saladin, strode to the center of the arena. Not far away from Mr. Saladin stood Mr. Codatorta, the school's self-defense teacher, always ready to protect the ancient headmaster.

"Welcome!" Mr. Saladin announced. "Welcome, all . . . to the unveiling of the new Redfountain!" The headmaster raised his dragon-headed staff, and a blast of power made his long gray hair whoosh around his head. *Surgat castellum!* he intoned.

With a deafening rumble, a huge cloud of dust rose. Headmaster Saladin glowed brightly while he concentrated, and the entirety of the school, all its castles and towers and landscaped grounds and gardens within its high walls, slowly lifted off the ground. It passed the tops of the trees until it was floating high in the clouds.

The crowd in the stadium bleachers went berserk with cheers and applause.

Now, *that* was an exciting surprise!

♥ ♥ ♥

Later that afternoon, the Winx, the four Specialists, and the Pixies relaxed in a shady garden in a Redfountain courtyard, lounging on the grass between tall trees. Nearby, Bloom was talking to Professor Avalon under a covered walkway.

"What a wonderful day it has been," the professor said. "Don't you think so, Bloom?"

Bloom nodded vigorously. "It was exciting," she agreed. "And I'm so glad you were here, Professor Avalon."

Sky stood up, scowling at Bloom and the professor. "It's like he's got her hypnotized," he grumbled. He was so focused on watching Bloom that he barely noticed a paper airplane sailing past his nose.

The paper airplane soared across the garden, heading over to Flora, who was sitting under a tree. It landed right beside her, and she picked it up.

"Oh," she murmured as she unfolded the plane. Inside was a lovely drawing—of her! Immediately, Flora knew who had made the picture. It could only have been Helia.

She hugged the drawing to her chest and giggled happily.

The next morning, Sky paced nervously around his bedroom at Redfountain, holding his cell phone. Finally, he stopped short and quickly made a call.

Bloom answered Sky's call at Alfea, where she was crossing the courtyard on her way to class, a stack of books under one arm. "Hey, Sky," she said cheerfully. "I had a great time yesterday."

"You mean with Professor Avalon?" asked Sky.

"Isn't he great?" gushed Bloom, oblivious to the jealous tone in Sky's voice. "I just love his class. We're learning so much. Hey, did I tell you that he's helping me visualize my past . . . to see my birth parents?"

"Oh, yeah," said Sky sarcastically.

Bloom narrowed her eyes. "What's that supposed to mean?"

"It means," Sky replied, "I'm a little sick of hearing you crush on the *great* professor."

"Crush on him?" demanded Bloom, losing her temper. "What is the *matter* with you?"

"I'm just calling it like I see it," said Sky.

"What?" Bloom shouted into her phone. She was

so upset by the conversation that she walked right into a wall and fell backward, dropping her books. "Ow!" she cried, sitting up with a groan and putting the phone back against her ear. "Listen, Sky," she said sulkily. "Do me a favor? Hang up the phone."

She listened for his reply, but to her total annoyance, he'd already hung up—before she'd even told him to!

Bloom stared sadly at her phone for a long moment and then flung it across the courtyard.

On the other side of Alfea, Flora sat near Aisha and Musa in Professor Palladium's charms class. Aisha and Musa were paying close attention to the orange-haired professor, but Flora was completely lost in a daydream.

Professor Palladium raised his slim green wand. "The key to an effective technical charm is proper pronunciation," he said.

"Oh," sighed Flora softly. "Helia . . ."

Aisha let out a little gasp when she overheard Flora's whisper.

"Now, in Elvish," Professor Palladium continued, "this spell is represented by this symbol. . . ."

Flora was lost in a fantasy. She imagined she was in a long, dark courtyard with poison-green walls, cowering on the floor as a grotesque eyeless monster cornered her, roaring and threatening with its claws.

Just when it was going to strike, powerful ropes launched toward the monster, entangling it. Helia was controlling the ropes, and he gave Flora a wink and a smile.

Then Flora imagined herself in a long, flowing gown. Helia was there, too, dressed in a fancy suit. He was carrying her in his arms down an aisle filled with flowers.

"Oh," Flora said, feeling as if she was going to swoon. "My hero."

Helia carried her to the altar, where a minister waited. The minister turned around.

Oddly, it was Professor Palladium. "Flora?" he asked loudly.

Flora blinked at him in confusion.

"Flora!" Professor Palladium repeated. "Flora!" He was no longer standing at the dreamy altar—now he was in front of his classroom, looking irritated.

Flora sat up sharply, dropping her pen. "Huh?" she gasped, disappointed that the dream had vanished.

It had been such a wonderful fantasy. . . .

After defeating the evil Trix and discovering her power of Dragon Flame, Bloom can't wait to start her second year at Alfea College for Fairies.

Bloom's best friend, Stella, plans to enjoy another year of friends and fashion!

Professor Avalon is a handsome and charming new teacher at Alfea—but he has a dark secret that could destroy all of Magix.

As Bloom falls under Professor Avalon's influence, Prince Sky becomes increasingly worried that the professor is not all he seems and that Bloom is in grave danger.

Banished to Lightrock Monastery after their failure to take over Magix, the evil Trix witches are powerless—until a dark creature called the Shadow Phoenix breaks them out. The Trix agree to help the Shadow Phoenix in his quest for power.

An exhausted pixie arrives at Alfea with terrible news: the Shadow Phoenix seeks a magical Codex hidden in Pixie Village that will give him the ultimate power!

The Shadow Phoenix sends Icy to Pixie
Village to retrieve the hidden Codex.
Using her diabolical powers, she succeeds
and brings it to the Shadow Phoenix.

But the Winx aren't about to let evil win the day! They are determined to defeat the Shadow Phoenix and prove that fairies rule once and for all!

Chapter 8

On the outskirts of the Alfea grounds, on the other side of a wide lake, Bloom swooped through the air, dressed in her battle outfit. She furiously hurled a fireball at a makeshift target range, blasting a stone outcropping into bits.

Professor Avalon stood nearby, watching Bloom practice her fiery abilities.

"Just calling it like he sees it," Bloom grumbled, still angry at Sky. "Right!" She tossed another fireball, smashing a rocky tower into smithereens. "Crushing on him!" she cried. Her whole body tensed with irritation as she blew up another boulder. "Oh!"

Bits of rock rained down, bouncing at Professor

Avalon's feet. "Bloom," he asked as she landed beside him, "what's going on?"

Bloom looked away, slightly ashamed of her explosive outburst. "Oh, nothing, really," she replied.

"That's not what it looks like," said the handsome teacher.

"Professor, it's Sky," admitted Bloom. "He's being . . . horrible!" Tears welled up in her eyes, and when Professor Avalon rested a sympathetic hand on her shoulder, she whirled around and buried her face against his chest, bursting into sobs.

Professor Avalon stroked her long scarlet hair. "Then perhaps you're better off without him," he said softly.

❤ ❤ ❤

Across Magix's lush forest, Sky sat on the edge of his bed in the room he shared with Brandon in the rebuilt Redfountain dorms. He had just finished his daily workout and had taken off his sweaty T-shirt.

While Sky called Bloom's number on his cell phone, Brandon did bicep curls with dumbbells on the other side of the room.

"It's still busy," groaned Sky, staring bleakly at his phone.

Brandon grunted, finishing another set of reps. "So she's not taking your calls, huh?" he asked.

Ignoring Brandon, Sky quickly called Bloom's number again. He sat up straighter when he heard a click on the other end but slumped in disappointment when he realized it was only a recorded message.

"Bloom can't come to the phone right now," said Bloom in her message, sounding rather irritated. "You may leave a message after the tone . . . but not if it's you, Sky."

Sky sighed. "Magic makes voice mail so frustrating!" he complained, tossing the phone onto his bed. Then he got up and walked past Brandon to their small balcony. Their room was located in one of the lower levels of the floating school, and the balcony provided an amazing panoramic view of the vast green forest below.

"Bloom," Sky muttered, leaning on the railing. Alfea was too far away through the woods to spot from Redfountain, but Sky peered into the distance anyway, wishing he could see the teenage fairy he cared for so deeply. "What is going on with you?"

A few rooms away on the same level of the Redfountain dorms, Helia sat cross-legged on his bed, meditating. He was trying to clear his mind so he could access deeper concentration and hone his powers, but he was distracted by a flurry of movement.

"Huh?" he murmured, getting up and going to the balcony. When he saw his potted rosebush growing wildly with intertwining vines and gorgeous yellow blossoms, he smiled and leaned down to inhale the lovely fragrance.

Helia glanced up and scanned the skies around Redfountain. He grinned when he caught sight of her—Flora was flying away, back toward Alfea. Only

she would be sweet enough to make my roses bloom like this! he thought.

Helia could almost hear Flora giggling happily as she swooped through the clouds on her way home.

In a shadowy office at Alfea, a tall man wearing a long blue robe swirled a toxic-looking green liquid in a glass flask. Foul smoke oozed out of the spout.

The man held up the vial and peered into the murky fluid, nodding with satisfaction. "And now for the Pixies," he growled, and turned around to pour the liquid into a big, bubbling cauldron in the middle of the dark office.

The stewing potion in the cauldron hissed and sizzled, glowing greener with eerie illumination. The robed man tossed in a handful of bone dust and added a mixture of rare dried herbs he'd collected from graveyards.

A cloud of sour smoke mushroomed out of the cauldron, followed by a burp of mystical fire.

"*Conorunam . . . expeditum . . . varum,*" the man intoned, and seven acid-green spheres bubbled up from the potion, floating in the air.

The robed man pointed sharply at a wall with his gloved hand. "Golem!" he ordered, and the spheres zoomed toward the wall. They didn't burst when they hit the stone—they passed right through as though the wall wasn't even there.

With an evil chuckle, the man lowered his dark blue hood.

It was Professor Avalon, and his laughter followed the toxic spheres as they bobbed down the corridors of Alfea.

The glowing spheres passed through a ceiling, then through the outside walls of the school, exiting into the gardens on the east side. They arrived near a maze of emerald hedges, where the Pixies were playing hide-and-seek.

Chatta peered up at the spheres through the visor on her helmet. "Huh?" she squeaked. "What—?"

The spheres zoomed down at Chatta and knocked the little Pixie off her feet.

Nearby, Tune and Amore were scampering through the hedge maze when the spheres popped out of the bushes. Both Pixies gasped in shock. The spheres zapped them unconscious and they slumped to the ground.

On the other side of the playground, Lockette let out a shriek as the spheres chased her toward a bandshell protected by a magical force field. She had almost reached safety when the spheres struck her with a painful green energy. The Pixie fell to the ground, unconscious.

♥ ♥ ♥

For the rest of the afternoon, no one at Alfea noticed that the Pixies had been attacked in the playground. Dusk fell, and one by one, the Pixies climbed to their feet. Their eyes swirled. They'd been hypnotized.

"Oh, my head," Lockette said in a flat voice, rubbing her temples. Then an overwhelming command echoed in her mind. "I must go back to

Pixie Village." She turned and started walking stiffly, like a zombie, in the direction of her secret home in the forest.

Watching through his scrying sphere from the throne room in his underground tower, the Shadow Phoenix let out a nasty laugh. He gloated as the other Pixies climbed to their feet in the Alfea playground, too.

"Exactly as planned," he said, pleased.

The sphere showed Chatta turning slowly so that she faced the same direction as Lockette. "Pixie Village," she peeped.

"We must get back to Pixie Village," added Amore.

All the Pixies started flapping their shimmering wings, taking to the air. "Pixie Village," they chirped robotically, flying in a loose squadron over the walls of Alfea. "We must go back to Pixie Village. Yes, Pixie Village!" Glittering Pixie dust trailed behind them. The moon shone full and large over the forest as they soared into the woods.

The Shadow Phoenix shook his head in dark amusement. "Those weaklings," he sneered, shutting

down his scrying sphere. He turned to face his huge, empty throne room. "Icy!" he called sharply. "Where are you?"

Icy instantly appeared, rising through the floor near the glowing brazier that lit the room. When she had fully risen, she bowed deeply, with only a hint of mockery. "You hollered, my lord?"

The Shadow Phoenix pointed at her with a sharp claw. "Follow the Pixies to Pixie Village," he ordered. He squeezed his claws into tight fists, shaking them in angry excitement. "Take the Codex from them and bring it to me."

"Very well," replied Icy. "I'm on it."

She sank back down, calmly vanishing into the stone floor.

The Shadow Phoenix allowed a tiny smile to twitch his lips. "The Codex is almost mine!"

Chapter 9

Icy summoned six hideous beasts to help her track the Pixies through the forest. The monsters she created looked like wolves mixed with rhinoceroses—they were ugly, mean, and fast, and they had sharp teeth and an excellent sense of smell. She flew after the creatures as they thundered through the woods, hot on the Pixies' trail.

Not far ahead, the Pixies floated along in their magical trance, twittering in unison, "We must go back to Pixie Village!" They were completely oblivious to the beasts' hooves pounding on their trail.

"Come on, you stupid monsters!" Icy urged the grotesque creatures as the Pixies came into view through the tall pine trees. "Move!"

Icy let out an evil laugh as she swooped ahead of

the beasts, impatient with their pace. The Pixies led her into a clearing, and Icy soared higher to get a better view of the little town she saw there. The settlement had a few miniature orange castles around a tiny fountain, along with squat little homes scattered like mushrooms. All through the town, a hundred small Pixies peered up at the witch, their faces frozen with worry.

"Pixie Village," sneered Icy. "How quaint. I think I'll destroy it."

She landed near the fountain, her enormous shadow looming over the whole town. The Pixies screamed in terror.

"Well, hello there," the witch said. "My name is"—she paused to raise her palms and blast the middle of the village with a burst of frozen energy—"Icy!" Snow swirled around the tiny streets, forming icicles on the buildings and freezing a few Pixies in place.

Other Pixies shrieked and rushed around, trying to escape, but a wall of ice formed on the outskirts of town, trapping them.

"I am here for the Codex!" Icy shouted. Her dark

blue cape whipped behind her in the snowy storm she'd created. "Where is it?"

The beasts that Icy had brought patrolled the village's borders, growling at any Pixies that tried to fly away.

Icy put her hands on her hips. "Give me the Codex," she said with fake sweetness, "or I'll turn you all into . . . *Pixie-sicles!*"

The Pixies squealed in fear but settled down when an older Pixie appeared in a yellow flash, floating in front of Icy's face. This Pixie had a dignified appearance, with a dome of golden hair held up by a jeweled tiara. She carried a staff with a glowing pearl on it. "I am Ninfea," she said. "What do you want, witch?"

"Have you not been listening?" Icy retorted. She raised her hands and a group of Pixies on the ground in front of her froze into chunks of ice. "Give me the Codex!"

"No!" Ninfea pleaded.

Icy bent down to glare at the teeny Pixie queen.

"If I don't get the Codex right now," she said, "I will destroy Pixie Village and every Pixie in it!"

At Icy's command, the rhino-wolves prowled closer, growling and threatening the cowering Pixies with their snapping jaws.

"No!" Ninfea screamed. "No, stop!" She fluttered down to the ground, and the pearl in her staff glowed brightly. Green sparkles flickered around the staff as Ninfea twirled it, muttering an incantation. The whole staff spun out of Ninfea's hand, transforming into an oval-shaped gray object with mystical symbols along its edges. It flipped toward Icy, who snatched it out of the air with her bony hand.

"The Codex!" said Icy, with a chilling smile. "The Phoenix will be so pleased."

♥ ♥ ♥

Icy wasted no time rushing back to the Shadow Phoenix's underground tower. She met with Darcy

and Stormy in front of the Shadow Phoenix's throne, where he sat under a giant statue of a snake.

"Finally," the Shadow Phoenix grumbled, "you're back."

"And with a little present," said Icy, smirking. She held out her hand and presented the Codex to the Shadow Phoenix.

He snatched it with a red claw. "At last!" he breathed, holding the oval object up to his face so he could peer at it closely. "The Codex." He closed his other hand in a tight fist. "And now . . . for the final part of my plan . . . Bloom and the Dragon Flame!"

The Shadow Phoenix's evil laughter echoed throughout his throne room.

A short while later, over at Alfea, Bloom, and Professor Avalon strolled along a bright, windowed hallway, chatting amicably.

"Bloom," said Professor Avalon, his hands clasped behind his back, "I feel there is more I can do to help

you find your birth parents. Are you willing to try again?"

"Oh, yes, Professor Avalon!" Bloom replied. She followed him into his classroom and took a seat in a chair near his desk. She looked up at her teacher's face.

"For this exercise, I need your absolute trust," said Professor Avalon. "Can you give it to me?"

"Yes, Professor," Bloom answered solemnly.

"Good," Professor Avalon said. He strode over to his desk and waved his hand, conjuring up a giant ball of glowing energy.

Bloom stood in surprise.

"Come with me," said Professor Avalon, gesturing toward the radiant teleportation sphere. Together they stepped through the shimmering portal and were instantly transported to a featureless realm of sickly yellow light.

Unable to see anything but the ugly milky energy, Bloom felt uncomfortable. She crossed her arms protectively. "Professor?" she asked. "What is this place?"

When he didn't answer immediately, Bloom glanced over at her teacher and was shocked to see his handsome face contorted in an expression of evil glee.

"Someplace where you cannot escape me!" answered Professor Avalon.

His horrible laughter echoed throughout the empty yellow realm.

♥ ♥ ♥

Meanwhile, in her office across Alfea's grounds, Headmistress Faragonda was meeting with Ninfea and other Pixies from Pixie Village, including the Pixies that had bonded with the Winx. The little Pixies all bobbed in the air in front of the fairy headmistress's wide desk.

"So you no longer have the Codex?" asked Miss Faragonda. The idea of the Codex being in the wrong hands caused her face to crease with serious concern.

"No!" Ninfea peeped in reply. "We had to give it to that witch, Icy!"

Miss Faragonda shook her head ruefully. "And she will give it to the Shadow Phoenix," she said. "With the Codex, the Shadow Phoenix can force open the doorway to the Interplanetary Dimension."

"Oh, no!" squealed Lockette.

Digit squeaked, "Disaster!"

Miss Faragonda nodded. "And if he had a source of great power—"

The office door banged open and Stella burst in, followed by Aisha, Musa, Tecna, and Flora. "Miss Faragonda!" Stella cried. "Bloom is missing!"

"Bloom!" gasped Lockette.

"We've been looking all over," Musa added.

Tecna poked at the screen of her handheld magical computer and then held it up for Miss Faragonda to see. "I've detected an unusual temporal disturbance in Professor Avalon's classroom," she said. "Here . . . I can translate it into an image." Tecna slid her finger across the gadget's screen and a hologram flickered in the air, hovering in front of the headmistress. An image appeared, fuzzy at first, then sharper. It showed Professor Avalon taking Bloom into the yellow

sphere . . . and then the sphere winking out of existence.

"Professor Avalon!" said Musa, stunned.

Horrified, Stella clapped her hands to her mouth. "He kidnapped Bloom!"

Even Headmistress Faragonda's eyes were wide behind her small glasses. "Our enemy was here all the time," she said, realizing the gravity of the situation. "And now he has the Dragon Flame. . . . That's all he needs to seize control of the Magic Dimension!"

Miss Faragonda took a deep breath, steadying herself. She narrowed her eyes in fierce determination. "Quickly, girls," she said. "We must stop the Shadow Phoenix and rescue Bloom."

Chapter 10

Headmistress Faragonda quickly contacted the Specialists for help, and Sky, Brandon, Timmy, Riven, and Helia rushed over to Alfea in a ruby-red spacecraft. Along with the Winx and the Pixies, they gathered around Miss Faragonda in the vast courtyard.

"Bloom is a prisoner of the Shadow Phoenix in his underground castle," Headmistress Faragonda told the group. "I am counting on the Winx and the Specialists to rescue her."

"We'll find her, Miss Faragonda," Stella promised.

Headmistress Faragonda nodded. She gestured for a few of the Pixies to fly closer to her. "You will not be alone," she told the Winx and the Specialists,

nodding to the four oldest Pixies, including Ninfea, who were hovering in front of her. "The Pixies have volunteered to accompany you. They can open the doorway to the Interplanetary Dimension." Miss Faragonda squared her shoulders as she peered through her glasses at the Winx fairies and the Specialists. "Hurry!" she said urgently. "There is no time to waste."

Everyone rushed aboard the Specialists' spaceship. The high-tech doors swirled closed behind them, and moments later, the ship rose from Alfea's courtyard with its antigravity engines. It zoomed into the night sky, away from the fairy college, soaring over the lake and the dark forests, blasting through clouds lit only by the moon.

Timmy piloted the ship back to the remote mountains where he had dropped off Bloom, Aisha, and Stella to rescue the Pixies. He steered the craft down and through a stone archway, easing it into a deep valley. "Hang on, everybody," he said. "We're entering the tunnels."

Standing behind Timmy's seat, Tecna peered over

his shoulder at the controls and monitors. "This is the most direct route to the Phoenix's castle," she said.

"True," Timmy replied, "but it's also the trickiest!" He gritted his teeth and flew the ship through giant rock tunnels that spiraled into the depths of the planet.

Aisha crossed the ship's bridge to stand near Stella and Brandon. "We need to be prepared to meet resistance," she warned. "The Shadow Phoenix has an army of shadow monsters."

Helia spun around in his chair to face the fairies. "That's what we're here for," he said, narrowing his eyes. The spaceship soared into the vast underground chamber that enclosed the Shadow Phoenix's giant stalagmite castle.

♥ ♥ ♥

Deep inside the twisted stone tower, Professor Avalon sat upon the Shadow Phoenix's throne, his

brilliant golden wings outstretched behind him. Standing in front of the dais was Bloom, her wrists and shoulders bound with magic cords that prevented her from using her powers.

"And now it is time for you to see me as I really am," he said. "Not your kind Professor Avalon, but"— in a flash, the handsome professor transformed into a grotesque red skeletal shape, his wings changing from golden feathers to dirty tatters of ripped skin—"the Shadow Phoenix!"

"You tricked me!" shouted Bloom. She struggled against the magic ropes, but they were too strong for her to break. "Why have you brought me here?"

The Shadow Phoenix stepped off the dais and strode closer to Bloom, his eyes glowing like scarlet embers. "Because with you, Fairy of Dragon Flame," he replied, "I will rule all of Magic Dimension!"

Bloom glared at him furiously. "That is never going to happen, Shadow Buzzard!"

"Excuse me," said a bored voice, and Icy sauntered into the throne room. She smiled in amusement at

the Shadow Phoenix's snarl of irritation at her sudden appearance. "Sorry to interrupt your little tête-à-tête," she said, not sounding sorry at all. "Master," she added as an afterthought.

Bloom's emerald eyes glittered with rage when she saw Icy, and then Darcy and Stormy close behind her. "The Trix!" she murmured angrily.

"What do you *want*?" the Shadow Phoenix snapped, climbing back up to his throne.

Stormy leaned against a pillar. "We thought you might like to know," she said, "that we're under attack."

"There's a shiny spaceship outside full of Specialists," said Darcy. "*And* the Winx." She lined up with the other two witches in front of the Shadow Phoenix's throne.

"A petty annoyance," the Shadow Phoenix growled. He raised his palm in a dismissive gesture. "You deal with it."

"What?" demanded Icy, shaking her fist. "That's it? We're on our own?"

The Shadow Phoenix paused a moment, thinking, and then smiled broadly at the Trix. "Gather my army," he commanded. "Give them your powers and let them do the fighting."

♥ ♥ ♥

Outside the castle in the Specialists' spaceship, Timmy slowed the craft to a stop. "We're in position," he announced.

"Everyone!" called Sky as he jumped up from his flight chair. "Battle stations!"

The other Specialists, the Winx, and the Pixies all prepared for the fight.

Below them, the Trix strode out of the castle and climbed a high, rocky cliff, getting ready for the battle themselves.

Inside the ship, Helia and Riven rode an elevator tube to the spacecraft's upper hull, and Sky hurried down to the shuttle decks. He hopped into one of the small, beetle-shaped battleships and zoomed through the sliding bay doors, which closed behind him.

Nearby, the Trix had reached the end of the rock

ledge that poked from the front of the stone tower. "Now!" Icy ordered.

The Trix concentrated as they focused on calling up their powers. Stormy's hands glowed with spiral galaxies of energy. Icy's power glowed green in a blaze between her palms. Darcy radiated ripples of electrical force as she conjured up a sphere that surrounded all three witches on the high rock.

The Trix's powers joined together, and the sphere turned bright purple. It expanded rapidly, growing until it filled the entire underground cavern with its malevolent energy.

All around the cavern, horrible mud-colored beasts opened their eyes, which shone with an evil red light. Packs of rhino-wolves lined up along the walkways and bridges around the castle and shot small purple power spheres out of their mouths at Sky's battle shuttle and the Specialists' main ship.

Several of the power spheres smacked into the ship, rocking it in the air. On the ship's bridge, the Winx and the Pixies screamed as they held on to chairs and computer equipment to steady themselves.

The rhino-wolves kept up the attacks, firing on

the ship with more power spheres that they spat out from their gullets.

"Starting evasive maneuvers!" shouted Timmy as he steered the ship behind a rocky pillar to avoid the attacks. He fired back at a group of rhino-wolves, blasting them off a bridge.

On the other side of the cavern, Sky zoomed along the edge of the rock wall, firing at a group of dinosaur-like beasts who were attacking from the ledges. The dino-beasts all heaved huge boulders at Sky's shuttle, but he managed to steer around the projectiles. As he flew past a ledge, one of the dino-beasts leapt and landed on top of his shuttle. The beast scrambled onto the windshield, clinging to the shuttle with its lower claws. It roared at Sky through the glass and pounded on the windshield with its fists.

CHAPTER
11

"I'm going to ditch this loser," said Sky. He turned the shuttle's controls hard, and his little ship careened wildly through the cavern. It was extremely difficult to steer with the shuttle turning and twisting, but Sky managed to avoid a pair of long stalactites, expertly threading between them.

The dino-beast still clung to the windshield, but it had stopped pounding on the glass. Now it only fought to hold on.

With the shuttle whirling so rapidly, Sky began to feel horribly dizzy. "Whoa!" he cried, fighting to stay conscious as the ship spun out of control, blasting down toward the lake far below.

As the shuttle reached the lake, Sky pulled the ship upward sharply—and the dino-beast finally lost

its grip. It flailed through the air and dropped into the water.

Sky struggled to regain control of the shuttle, gritting his teeth. "Got to level her out," he panted, barely managing to keep the shuttle from dashing into the rocks that made up the castle's tower. One of the shuttle's wings was sputtering with sparks, and clouds of greasy smoke trailed from the damaged circuits.

"Sky!" Riven hollered over the shuttle's communicator. "We're right above you!"

With a quick glance out his windshield, Sky spotted the big spacecraft hovering over his wobbly shuttle. "Nice to see you," he replied. "Positioning for docking."

Riven focused carefully on lowering the big ship closer to the shuttle. "Roger that," he said, and pressed a button that opened the wide bay doors on the spacecraft's underside.

Trying desperately to compensate for his shuttle's wonky balance, Sky aimed for the landing bay, but the shuttle was veering too much to dock. "My left

rudder is gone," he reported frantically. "I can't level my approach."

In the spacecraft's upper deck, Riven wildly pressed buttons on his control panels, trying anything that might help Sky dock safely. But he couldn't match the ship's movements to the shuttle's unpredictable wobbling. "He's in trouble!" Riven told Helia, who was sitting in the seat next to him. "He's not going to make it."

Sky heroically kept trying to enter the bay doors, but he couldn't keep the shuttle level, no matter how he maneuvered it.

Helia glanced at Riven. "I'll reel him in," he said, and leapt out of his chair. It only took him a few seconds to reach the landing bay. He smiled as he stood solidly in the center of the docking area, pleased with the opportunity to use his magical powers.

With a flick of his wrist, Helia launched a glowing cord that seemed to come straight out of his hand. The cord wriggled toward Sky's shuttle, extending until it looped around the craft's nose and fastened itself securely.

Helia grunted as he set his feet and pulled against the glowing cord with all his might. For a moment, it seemed as though his efforts were working. Sky's shuttle leveled out and started heading into the spacecraft through the open bay doors.

Just then, a flurry of flying shadow monsters swooped down at the shuttle, smacking it with their wings and raking it with their claws. The shuttle floundered, losing altitude sharply, and Helia fell, flopping onto his stomach and sliding across the floor as the falling shuttle started to drag him out of the docking bay.

With a shout of defiance, Helia pulled himself to a sitting position and managed to catch the edge of the bay doorway with the heels of his boots. His face twisted with effort as he yanked on the glowing cord, hoisting the shuttle back up to the level of the bay doors. He pulled hard on the cord and then jumped back as the shuttle suddenly shot into the spacecraft.

The shuttle slid safely to a stop, perfectly in its place in the docking bay.

Up on the bridge, Timmy cheered, "Helia got him!"

Helia smiled, retracting his magical cord.

"In our final approach," Riven reported from the upper deck as he steered the spacecraft around the center shaft of the Shadow Phoenix's stalagmite castle.

Brandon peered at the fairies across the bridge from his copilot spot. "Okay, Winx," he said, "time to go into action. We'll finish off the monsters."

The teenage fairies gathered in a tight circle at the center of the bridge. "You ready?" asked Tecna, clenching one hand into a fist.

"Yes!" the other Winx replied.

"Let's transform!" Tecna hollered.

"Magic Winx!" shouted Stella, Flora, Musa, Tecna, and Aisha together. "Charmix!"

A blaze of multicolored magical energy blasted through the bridge, encircling the Winx. Each fairy was surrounded by a brilliant swirl of mystical force that filled her with intense power and changed her into her battle form, with a sleek outfit and shimmering wings.

One by one, they called out their names and powers as the transformation reached a fever pitch.

"Tecna! Fairy of Technology!"

"Musa! Fairy of Music!"

"Stella! Fairy of the Shining Sun!"

"Flora! Fairy of Nature!"

"Aisha! Fairy of the Waves!"

As the Specialists' spaceship made a final circuit of the castle, the bay doors opened again and the powered-up Winx soared out into the cavern, followed by their Pixie friends. They zoomed into the castle, entering through the basement dungeons and flying through the corridors into the dark heart of the Shadow Phoenix's lair.

"Come on, Winx!" called Stella.

Aisha soared through the corridors with her friends. "Let's find Bloom!"

"Yeah!" the Pixies shouted together.

In the Shadow Phoenix's throne room, Bloom struggled wearily against her glowing magical

bindings as the red skeletal creature floated over to her.

"Now my plan will finally be complete," the Shadow Phoenix said. "I will have ultimate power, with the Codex and the Dragon Flame . . . when you, fairy, become"—he raised his hand, and swirls of black and purple energy churned on his palm—"Dark Bloom!"

The Shadow Phoenix launched the twisting power directly at Bloom. The force swarmed toward her, flickering with mystical symbols.

"No!" cried Bloom as the painful energy slammed into her. The purple and black sank into her skin, sending shocks of evil lightning throughout her body. Bloom shuddered wildly as she transformed into a creature of darkness. Her emerald eyes burned with a wicked light, changing color to resemble the yellow eyes of a lizard. Her bonds fell away. She floated in the air in a glimmering green outfit, wide white wings fluttering behind her and a fiendish smile playing on her lips.

The Shadow Phoenix let out a booming laugh

when he saw the success of the plan he'd worked so long to achieve. He held out his claw to Dark Bloom, and she took his sharp fingers in her hand.

"Come, my dear," the Shadow Phoenix said, leading Dark Bloom across the throne room. "We will begin the ritual."

When they reached a low cabinet, the Shadow Phoenix carefully placed the Codex in an ornate box with no top.

"We're almost ready, Dark Bloom," he told her. Dark Bloom giggled maliciously.

The Trix rushed into the throne room and stood in front of the Shadow Phoenix and Dark Bloom with their hands on their hips, scowling in irritation.

"Leaving so soon?" sneered Darcy.

"Aren't you forgetting something?" asked Icy.

"Like, say, *us*?" added Stormy.

The Shadow Phoenix let out a low chuckle. "No, I haven't forgotten. I know you want a share of the power that will soon be mine." He peered at the teen witches. "But that's not part of the plan!"

With a sudden hand gesture, the Shadow Phoenix

slammed scarlet spirals of power into Icy. She was blasted backward onto the floor.

Stormy and Darcy gasped in surprise.

"I send you back from where you came," the Shadow Phoenix declared. Crimson lightning danced from his claws, ripping a teleportation portal in the air. "Lightrock Monastery!"

Dark Bloom laughed as the Shadow Phoenix waved his hand and the portal sucked the Trix in. The witches shrieked as they tumbled across the room and swirled into the portal, which vanished in a flash.

The Shadow Phoenix shared a cruel smile with Dark Bloom. "And now," he said, "we will begin."

Chapter 12

"I can sense Bloom," squealed Lockette, pointing down a dark corridor in the Shadow Phoenix's castle. "Come on, this way!" She fluttered down the hall in a shimmer of glittering sparkles, followed by the other Pixies. The Winx strode along the corridor after their tiny friends.

Stella paused for a moment to peer down another hallway that led in a different direction. She shivered a little as she resumed walking with the Winx and the Pixies. "You know," she murmured, "I've got a feeling we're not alone."

The wall beside Flora suddenly trembled and cracked open. Chunks of marble and rock crumbled onto the floor of the corridor, dropping around Flora's pink boots.

"What is going on?" cried Flora.

Then a tall, muscular blue monster wearing a leather hood sprang through the hole in the wall. It had smashed through with its enormous double-headed axe. The beast snarled furiously at the Winx.

Stella immediately flung a fireball at the monster, but it smacked the ball back with its axe. The fireball sizzled over to the Winx, knocking them out of the air. The fairies crashed into the rubble on the floor.

Aisha covered her face with her forearm, wincing in pain. "Right in my eye!" she cried. "I can't see!" She has been temporarily blinded.

Flora hopped to her feet and glared angrily at the beast. "Roots and vines the monster will bind!" she intoned, casting a spell. At her command, thick green and brown shoots pushed up through the stone tiles of the floor and twisted toward the beast, trying to entwine him.

The shadow monster growled, swung his axe, and sliced the vines into tiny, useless chunks.

"All right," Musa declared, jumping in front of Flora. "Sound waves!" She leaned forward and placed

her hand on the floor. Concentric purple circles swirled out from her fingertips and radiated through the stone toward the beast.

The whole corridor trembled with the power of Musa's musical attack, but the monster only shrugged, unaffected.

"Drat," said Musa.

The beast raised his massive axe over its head and slammed it into the stone floor. A crack appeared where the monster had struck, unzipping the stone tiles toward the Winx. The vibrations were so intense that the fairies were blasted backward. They slammed into the wall hard enough to leave chips in the marble and slumped to the floor, dazed.

With a battle cry, the monster shook its axe at the fairies.

The Pixies hovered in front of their fairy friends, urging them to escape while they had a chance.

"Run!" Digit yelled.

The Winx climbed wearily to their feet and hurried down the corridor.

"We'll find a way to beat it!" shouted Musa.

The monster was faster than the Winx had

expected, though, and it quickly caught up with them in the hallway. The fairies cowered against a wall as the beast threatened them with its glinting weapon.

An older witch suddenly materialized in the corridor between the Winx and the monster and instantly zapped the giant with a stream of sizzling purple power. *"Captis obscurum!"* she cried.

It was Miss Griffin, the headmistress of the witches' college, Cloudtower! Right behind her were Mr. Codatorta, the weapons instructor from Redfountain, and Headmistress Faragonda.

The Winx had never been more thrilled to see anybody in their lives!

Miss Griffin's magical attack blasted the monster off its cloven hooves, and it slammed backward down the corridor, knocked out.

The fairies rushed over to the teachers and happily called out their names.

"Are we ever glad to see you!" said Musa.

Miss Faragonda smiled at her students. "Did you think we would not come to help?" she asked, gently teasing.

"B-but . . . ," sputtered Musa, pointing at the

beast. It was groaning as it regained consciousness.

"Oh, that?" said Mr. Codatorta. "Don't worry about it! We'll handle—"

But before the teacher could finish his sentence, the beast stood up and thrust its palm toward its opponents. To Mr. Codatorta's surprise, the monster launched a blast of brilliant force down the hall, smacking everyone to the floor. Then it stomped closer, wielding its enormous axe.

Mr. Codatorta hopped back up and helped Miss Griffin to her feet. "Lady Griffin, are you all right?" he asked.

"Fine," she replied, turning to face the approaching beast.

Miss Faragonda pulled herself to her knees and reached out to grab Aisha's hands. "Hurry, girls!" she said. "You must find Bloom!"

"Before the Shadow Phoenix completes his evil plan!" Ninfea added. The Pixie leader fluttered urgently down the corridor. "This way!"

Chapter 13

The Pixies and the Winx raced after Ninfea, rushing to keep up. The moment they were gone, the teachers turned to face the massive beast.

Miss Griffin glowed dark purple while Miss Faragonda radiated light green energy all around her. As the shadow monster swung its axe, the two headmistresses blasted the beast with their magical attacks. This time, the monster didn't fall, but it seemed dazed.

Mr. Codatorta lunged forward, wielding his broad crystal sword. He swung at the beast, then ducked as the monster swiped its axe over his head. The next time the giant attacked, Mr. Codatorta caught the axe blade with the flat edge of his sword, holding

the monster off. In an incredible display of force, he managed to push the beast back.

The monster jumped and swung its axe again, knocking the sword out of Mr. Codatorta's grip. The crystal blade clattered as it bounced away down the hall.

Miss Faragonda stepped forward, glowing with green energy. "Strength from the Ancient Titans!" she shouted, and a sphere of power shot from her and radiated into Mr. Codatorta, boosting his muscles.

"Speed of the Cheetah!" cried Miss Griffin, bathing Mr. Codatorta in purple intensity.

Mr. Codatorta radiated otherworldly energy as he leapt at the beast.

The shadow monster swung its axe at Mr. Codatorta, but the powered-up professor caught the blade between his palms. He wrenched the axe out of the beast's hands and tossed it away. Then, with breathtaking speed, he jumped forward and wrapped his bulging arms around the monster's waist.

Mr. Codatorta squeezed with all his might, and the shadow monster exploded in a cloud of foul darkness, dissipating like smoke.

Miss Griffin and Miss Faragonda exchanged satisfied smiles as Mr. Codatorta brushed dust off his tunic.

"Now that was a workout," said Mr. Codatorta.

Miss Faragonda peered at him over her glasses, her eyes glittering. "And now," she said, "the Shadow Phoenix."

Outside the castle, the Specialists battled the remaining shadow monsters that blocked the entrance to the Shadow Phoenix's lair.

"Here, monster, monster," Brandon said, taunting the evil creatures. He held his glowing green sword out in front of him as a dino-beast lurched at him, snapping with its vicious teeth.

Brandon whacked the creature on its leg and then leapt onto its head to deliver a knockout blow.

Nearby, Helia backed down a stone staircase as a dino-beast stomped toward him. "We need to wrap this up!" he yelled, but before he could attack the

monster, his boot slipped on a step and he tumbled down the stairs, landing hard on his back.

Sensing an advantage, the dino-beast lunged at Helia.

But even on his back, Helia wasn't defenseless. Before the monster could reach him, he shot four glowing golden cords from the back of his hand. The cords wrapped around the dino-beast, scorching it with dazzling energy. It fell with a thump beside Helia on the ground, out cold.

"That's it!" declared Sky, rushing up to Brandon. "Let's go!"

The Specialists sprinted into the castle entrance, running along corridors to find the Winx and help defeat the Shadow Phoenix in any way they could.

In the Shadow Phoenix's throne room, Dark Bloom placed the ornate box holding the Codex on a jade-green altar.

"And now, dear Dark Bloom," the Shadow

Phoenix said, "we will open the doorway to the Interplanetary Dimension."

Once the box had been placed on the altar, green sparkles began to shimmer around the Codex.

"And the Codex is the key," the Shadow Phoenix continued.

The Codex slowly rose out of the box, floating in the air. When it was just above Dark Bloom's eye level, it multiplied into four glowing ovals hovering above the altar in a row.

The Shadow Phoenix chuckled in anticipation as the four Codices swirled toward each other, whirling in an intricate pattern. They flew faster and faster until they were just a blur, creating a wind that whipped Dark Bloom's long scarlet hair.

The bright blur of the Codices became more intense and expanded as the color shifted from green to purple, spinning open into a mysterious tunnel of light that gaped into the unknown.

"Ah, here we are," the Shadow Phoenix breathed. "The Dimensional Passage!" He turned his head to smile at Dark Bloom. "Shall we?" he asked.

Dark Bloom nodded, and they strode into the blinding purple light of the open portal. The portal closed behind them as though it had never existed.

The Shadow Phoenix and Dark Bloom found themselves at the other end of the interdimensional passageway on a large rock floating in a hazy emptiness. The top of the rock was tiled with paving stones and surrounded by tall pillars, some intact and some broken. In the center of the rock, a small pyramid temple loomed up between the pillars.

Dark Bloom strode to the middle of the paving stones, surveying the area with satisfaction.

"Everything is set," the Shadow Phoenix said. "It is time for the ritual. Dark Bloom, begin the chant of power."

"Yes," replied Dark Bloom with a smile. She levitated onto the top of a broken pillar at the edge of the rock and stared out into the cloudy void surrounding them. *"Beatus fortis subvertio!"* she intoned, raising her arms as she began to shine with purple energy.

"That's it!" the Shadow Phoenix urged. "Keep going!"

"Beatus fortis subvertio!" Dark Bloom repeated, closing her eyes as she increased the intensity of the spell.

♥ ♥ ♥

Meanwhile, the Winx were racing as fast as they could through the castle's halls toward its dark heart. The Pixies flew along beside them, occasionally circling the fairies' heads as they ran.

"Hurry!" Ninfea cried. "To the throne room!"

With a final turn down a corridor, the Winx and the Pixies finally reached the seat of the Shadow Phoenix's power. They gathered around the dais in front of the empty throne.

Aisha peered up at the horrible giant snake looming over the throne. "This must be the place," she said.

"Then where's Bloom?" asked Stella.

The four Pixies of the Codex fluttered forward. "They must have already passed through the doorway," said Concorda, the oldest of the elders. "We can open it again for you."

Circling around the dais, the four elder Pixies took their places, floating in the air. *"Naperi ianua ut transeamus!"* the Pixies of the Codex chanted in unison. A purple portal swirled open between them.

"Let's go!" cried Aisha, and she bolted through the interdimensional opening, followed by the Winx and their Pixie friends.

In the other realm, Dark Bloom floated above the pyramid temple, her eyes narrowed in fierce concentration as she cast the spell to complete the Shadow Phoenix's evil ritual. *"Beatus fortis subvertio!"* she continued to chant, her skin glowing with raw power.

"Yes!" the Shadow Phoenix crowed. "The doorway is opening!"

At that moment, the other Winx zoomed through the interdimensional portal, buzzing across the floating rock on their strong wings.

"Not with us here to lock it down!" yelled Stella.

Chapter 14

"What?" the Shadow Phoenix growled as Stella and Aisha soared over to Dark Bloom floating above the temple pyramid.

"Plasma Warp!" yelled Aisha, and a watery sphere appeared between her outstretched hands.

Stella conjured up a glowing orange ball of force. "Solar Power!" she shouted.

Aisha and Stella aimed their attacks at the Shadow Phoenix, but as their blasts passed Dark Bloom, they knocked her off balance.

"Oh!" Dark Bloom gasped, tumbling down onto the pyramid.

At the same time, Flora, Musa, and Tecna zapped

the Shadow Phoenix with a coordinated attack of green streams of light.

"Take that!" Tecna hollered.

The Shadow Phoenix shot into the air, rising above the Winx's magic. Then he soared toward the fairies with a furious roar.

"Uh-oh," said Musa.

Dark Bloom tried to pull herself onto the top of the pyramid temple. The Shadow Phoenix landed beside her.

"Dark Bloom," he gasped, checking her for injuries. She was hurt, but would survive . . . and the Shadow Phoenix glared at the Winx with rage in his red eyes.

"Leave her alone!" Aisha yelled at him.

The Shadow Phoenix helped Bloom to her feet. "Start the chant over," he ordered. "I'll take care of them." He launched himself off the pyramid, zooming toward the Winx. "I'm going to make you very sorry, fairies!" he roared.

The Winx landed on the tops of the broken

pillars, preparing to battle the Shadow Phoenix. Stella launched a sunny blast at the red demon, calling to her friends, "We have to take him on together!"

Nodding, Aisha conjured up her own watery attack. Both her magic and Stella's reached the Shadow Phoenix at the same time, but he blocked them with a glowing shield.

"Pathetic," he sneered. He fought back with rapid, blistering blasts of his own, knocking the Winx off their pillars.

The fairies crashed to the ground, groaning in pain.

Suddenly, the Specialists sprinted through the portal behind the Shadow Phoenix. Brandon arrived first, followed by Sky, Timmy, Riven, and Helia.

"Hey, you!" Brandon hollered. "Leave them alone!"

"Release Bloom, Shadow Phoenix!" Sky demanded.

The Shadow Phoenix floated high above the temple, glaring at the young Specialists. "You didn't

say please, boy!" he growled angrily. Then he raised his hand and a purple shock wave shot out, slamming the Specialists to the floor beside the Winx.

Sky wriggled in the painful purple glow that surrounded him. "I can't move," he gasped.

A terrifying red glint glistened in the Shadow Phoenix's eyes. "The doorway is opening," he told the Specialists and the fairies. "And you are doomed!" He hovered closer to Dark Bloom, who had resumed her chanting.

"*Beatus fortis subvertio!*" repeated Dark Bloom, floating off the temple, her arms radiant with evil energy. "*Beatus fortis subvertio!*"

"Bloom!" Sky screamed in horror. "Bloom, no!"

But Dark Bloom had finished her spell. She stuck her arms straight up in the air as a terrifying whirlwind of concentrated sinister power appeared above her. She grinned and giggled, staring up at the ominous, pulsing mass of force she'd created in the sky.

With a chilling laugh, the Shadow Phoenix ran across the stone tile and leapt into the air. He

transformed into his fiery bird form as he flapped his wings of crimson flames. The Shadow Phoenix circled around Dark Bloom, soaring above her to drink in the tremendous energy she was producing. Sizzling bolts arced from the center of the source as the Shadow Phoenix absorbed the power.

"Oh, no!" Stella and Flora cried together. "Bloom!"

Flashes of sickening force blasted the Winx and the Specialists, but Sky couldn't give up—not when the girl he cared for so deeply was in such terrible danger. He shakily climbed to his feet and gritted his teeth as he inched closer to the mass of blazing energy Dark Bloom was making.

"Sky!" Brandon cried, trying to warn his friend.

But Sky was determined to help Bloom however he could. He had to get through to her—somehow. "Bloom, you've got to listen to me," he pleaded. "It's Sky. *Your* Sky!"

Dark Bloom's eyes twitched, but she returned to her efforts at maintaining the mass of ultimate energy the Shadow Phoenix was absorbing.

The Shadow Phoenix raised his grotesque bird's

head. "Do you think she still cares?" he mocked Sky. "Fool!"

Ignoring the demon bird, Sky focused his aquamarine eyes on Dark Bloom's beautiful face. "I want you to listen to me," he begged. "Listen to me and fight. Fight for who you truly are!"

A memory flickered between them: a wonderful moment when they'd touched fingertips while sitting in the sunlight outside Alfea, both shocked by the intensity of their connection.

"Fight for us," Sky continued to plead. "You are strong . . . stronger than the Shadow Phoenix and his evil. You saved my life once . . . now listen to me and save your own! I care more about you than anyone else in the entire world."

For a second, it looked as though Dark Bloom's harsh features were softening. Sky redoubled his efforts. "Please . . . please come back to me."

Sky reached out to Dark Bloom, but she sneered and conjured up a nimbus of purple energy around him. The energy flared hot, blasting him, and he crumpled, trembling in pain.

Still Sky wouldn't give up. "Bloom," he moaned, reaching up for her weakly.

As his friends looked on in horror, Sky slumped onto the stone ground, unconscious.

Chapter 15

Above Dark Bloom, the Shadow Phoenix cackled and flapped his glowing wings. With no more opposition, he settled in to devour all the energy Dark Bloom could create.

"At long last," he crowed, opening his beak to drink deep, "the sweet taste of—"

Suddenly, the taste of the energy changed. It *burned*.

"What?" the Shadow Phoenix gasped. "What's happening?"

Below him, Dark Bloom glowed white-hot, and with a brilliant flash, she changed back into her fairy form! Bloom concentrated deeply, summoning all her might as her eyes changed from lizard-yellow

back to emerald-green. She pulled the mass of energy out of the air, lowered it, and absorbed all the force into herself.

"What's this?" the Shadow Phoenix shrieked, flapping his wings in fury. "What's going on? It cannot be! It is impossible! No! For this, you will suffer!"

Bloom calmly lowered herself to the ground just as Sky was standing up again. She threw herself into his arms, hugging him.

"Bloom!" he cried happily, holding her in a warm embrace.

She buried her face in his broad shoulder. "Sky," she replied.

Before the Shadow Phoenix could begin his revenge, Mr. Codatorta, Miss Faragonda, and Miss Griffin jumped through the interdimensional portal and hurried to the students.

"Specialists!" Mr. Codatorta ordered. "Form up!"

The Shadow Phoenix opened his wings wide, menacing them from above. "I will destroy you all!" he screeched.

The Specialists dropped into ready positions. Timmy pulled out his laser blaster, Brandon activated his double-sided energy sword, and Sky conjured up a power shield and a sword.

"Shield the Winx!" called Sky.

Behind the Specialists, Miss Griffin smiled at the fairy headmistress. "Ready, Faragonda?" she asked.

Miss Faragonda grinned back at the fierce witch. "Of course, Griffin," she replied.

The Shadow Phoenix squawked loudly, spewing vicious purple balls of energy at the Winx.

The Specialists leapt in front of the fairies. Protecting Musa, Riven knocked the balls out of the air with his glowing sword, while Brandon spun his sword around so fast, they created a whirling barrier in front of Stella. Sky shielded Bloom, grinning in excitement.

"Go for it!" Brandon shouted. "We've got you covered!"

"Go on, Bloom," Sky urged.

The Shadow Phoenix let out a giant roar, infuriated that his attack had been blocked. He dove toward

the professors, screaming, "Welcome to oblivion!" Then he opened his beak, and out gushed a torrent of orange flame.

Working together, Miss Griffin and Miss Faragonda intoned, *"Supernus!"* A bright green dome appeared around the group, protecting them all from the Shadow Phoenix's fire.

The headmistresses grunted as they struggled to maintain their shield under the pressure of the Shadow Phoenix's powerful blast.

"Girls!" Miss Faragonda shouted at the Winx. "Now!"

Behind their teacher, the Winx joined hands in a tight circle, connecting their powers.

"Okay, Winx," said Bloom. "All together now."

The Winx closed their eyes, concentrating on combining their different strengths and abilities to form a more powerful, coherent whole. They knitted their brows, focusing on casting a spell stronger than any of them had ever attempted before.

"Charmix Convergence!" they shouted in unison. "Overload!"

A golden radiance emanated from the fairy circle, growing in intensity and size until it was blindingly brilliant.

"It's not possible!" the Shadow Phoenix howled. "No, no, *no!*"

But the Winx's energy wave kept growing, until at last the purity of its golden glow overwhelmed the Shadow Phoenix and he withered under its engulfing glare.

The Shadow Phoenix vanished in a blaze of glorious light. As his power broke, they all were teleported instantly to the throne room, just as the whole enormous underground cavern began to shudder and shake. Tremors shook the stone tower, and giant boulders tumbled down into the lake far below the castle.

"Are you okay?" Chatta asked when she saw the Winx and the Specialists pop out of the portal.

"Yes," Miss Faragonda replied, "and the Shadow Phoenix is no more."

Bits of marble and woodwork crumbled overhead as vibrations shook the castle.

"Everything is collapsing!" Concorda warned.

"Quick!" called Sky. "To the ships!"

Bloom jumped into action, racing out of the throne room. "Come on!"

They made it to the spacecraft just in time to flee the tumbling rock of the cavern's collapse.

That night, the courtyard at Alfea shimmered with a joyous celebration. Dozens of glowing spheres bobbed over the grounds, giving the college a mystical atmosphere for the exuberant party.

Watching from one of the main castle's marble balconies, Miss Faragonda and Miss Griffin clinked their glasses together in a toast and sipped their punch in satisfaction.

Down amid the revelry, Sky announced, "It's almost time!" Then he hurried up a flight of stairs. He found Bloom petting her adorable pet bunny, Kiko.

"Bloom!" he called. "There you are."

When Sky reached her, he stopped short and stared into her emerald eyes with his own aquamarine ones. They paused for a moment, lost in emotion, before moving together for a tight hug . . . and a tender kiss.

Behind Bloom, Lockette watched and giggled, blushing.

"Gather round, everybody!" Timmy shouted. "Picture time! Come on, all together!"

"You heard him, guys!" said Sky.

"Okay, that's it," Timmy said, gesturing to the group from behind the magical floating camera he was setting. "Move in a little bit."

"Come on," Sky told Bloom, "let's go." Holding hands, they raced down the stairs toward their friends on the lawn.

"Okay," said Timmy, dashing around the camera to be part of the picture. "The timer is set for ten seconds."

"Hurry up!" said Stella. "Everyone here?"

Sky and Bloom reached the group just as the camera flashed, forever capturing them running in front of all their cheering friends.